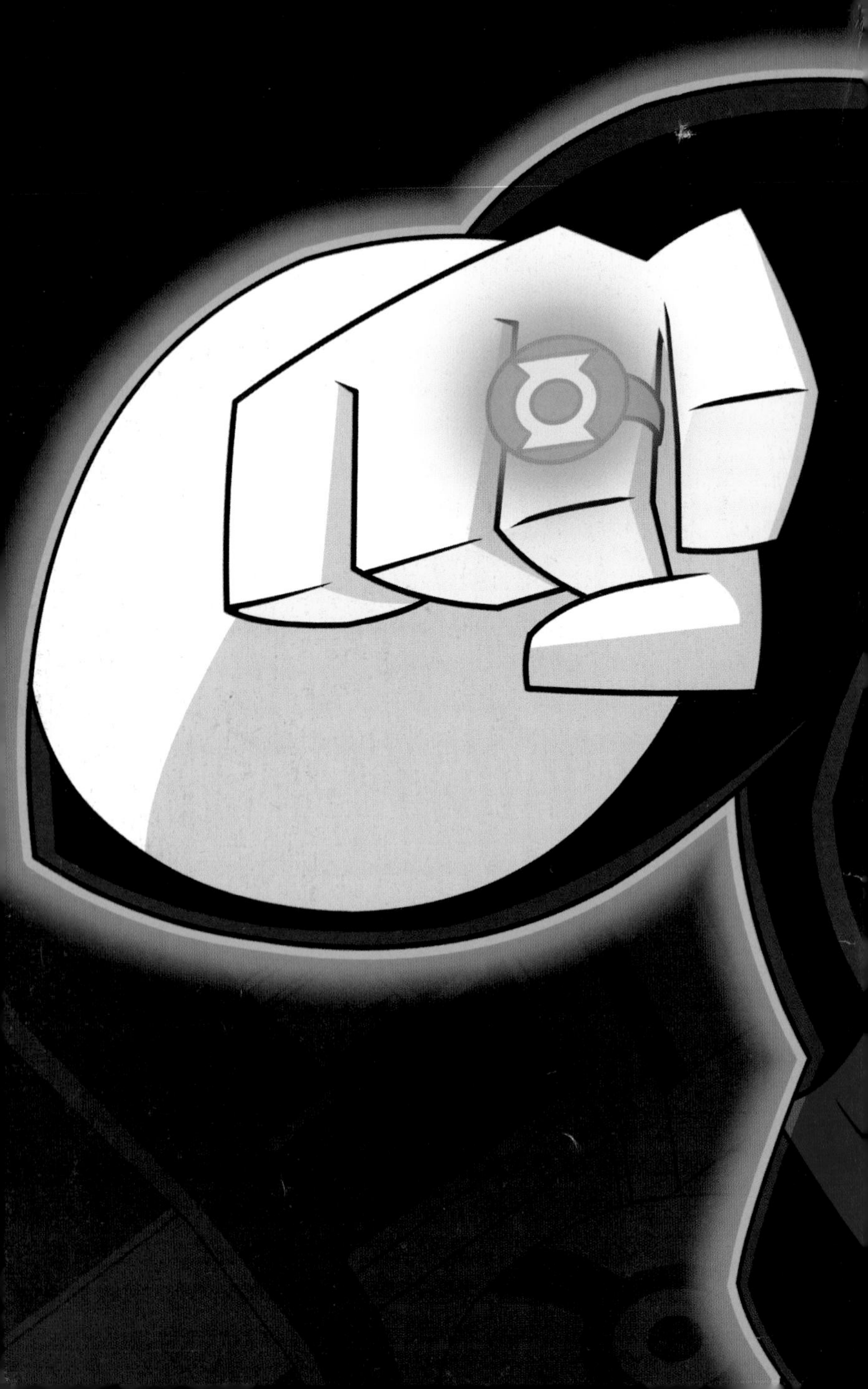

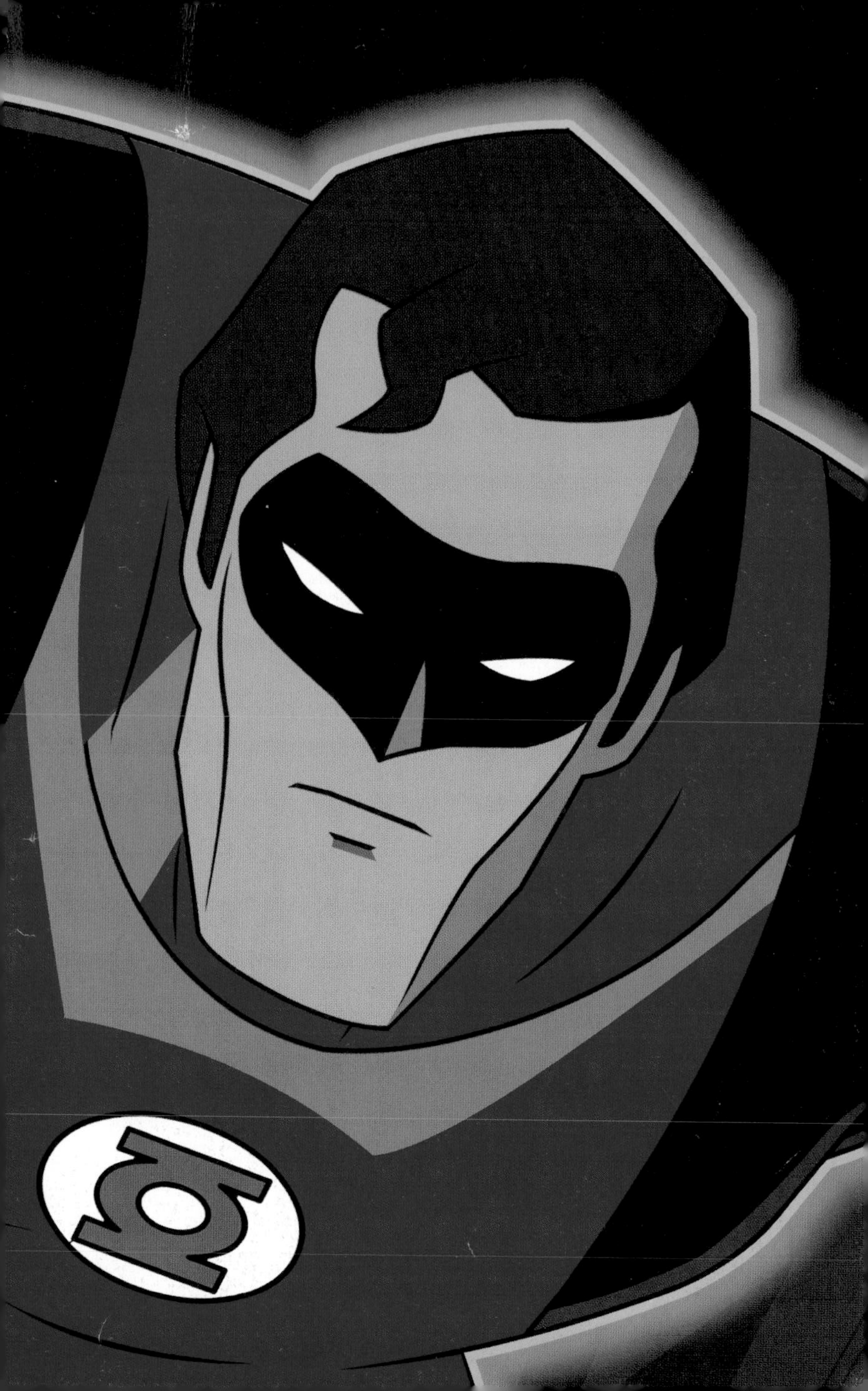

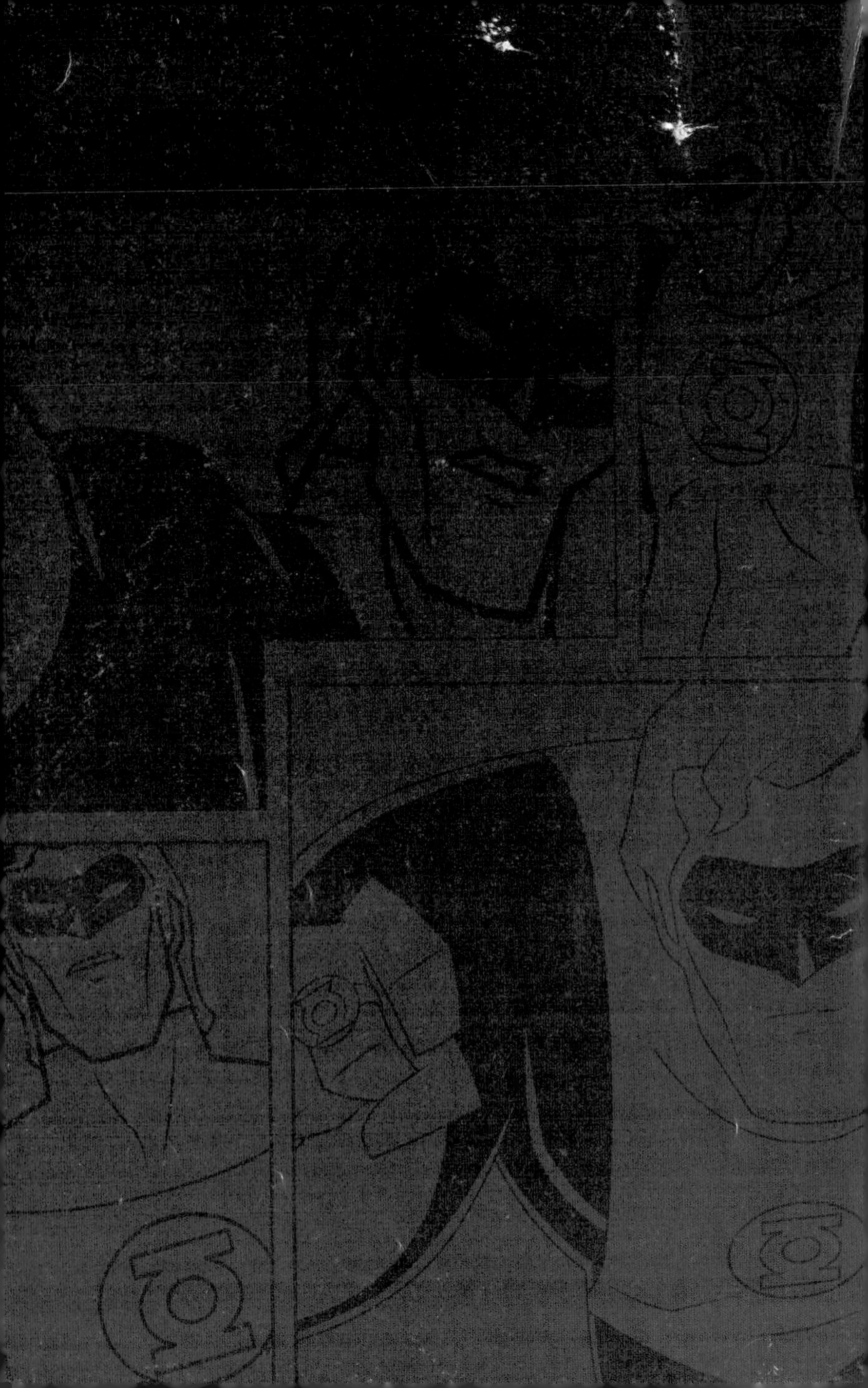

AS THE NEWEST MEMBER OF AN INTERGALACTIC PEACEKEEPING FORCE KNOWN AS THE GREEN LANTERN CORPS, HAL JORDAN FIGHTS EVIL AND PROUDLY WEARS THE UNIFORM AND RING OF . . .

SUPER DC HEROES

GREEN LANTERN

RED LANTERNS' REVENGE

WRITTEN BY
MICHAEL ACAMPORA

ILLUSTRATED BY
DAN SCHOENING

STONE ARCH BOOKS
a capstone imprint

Published by Stone Arch Books in 2012
A Capstone Imprint
151 Good Counsel Drive, P.O. Box 669
Mankato, Minnesota 56002
www.capstonepub.com

Library of Congress Cataloging-in-Publication Data
Acampora, Michael Vincent, 1989-
  Red Lanterns' revenge / written by Michael Acampora ; illustrated by Dan
Schoening.
     p. cm. -- (DC super heroes)
  ISBN-13: 978-1-4342-2623-5 (library binding)
  ISBN-13: 978-1-4342-3409-4 (pbk.)
  1. Green Lantern (Fictitious character)--Juvenile fiction. 2. Superheroes--
Juvenile fiction. 3. Supervillains--Juvenile fiction. [1. Superheroes--Fiction. 2.
Supervillains--Fiction. 3. Youths' writings. 4. Science fiction.] I. Schoening,
Dan, ill. II. Title.
  PZ7.A17298Re 2012
  [Fic]--dc22   2011005151

Summary: Hal Jordan travels to Mars with two Green Lantern Corps
teammates to investigate an explosion on the Red Planet. Several clues lead
them to the distant planet Ysmault, but it's a trap! Hal's companions are
captured by Atrocitus, leader of the rebellious Red Lanterns. But if Hal gives
in to his anger, the mad Atrocitus will grow in strength, take over Earth's solar
system, and become even more powerful than Hal!

Art Directors: Bob Lentz and Brann Garvey
Designer: Hilary Wacholz
Production Specialist: Michelle Biedscheid

Printed in the United States of America in Stevens Point, Wisconsin.
082011
006341R

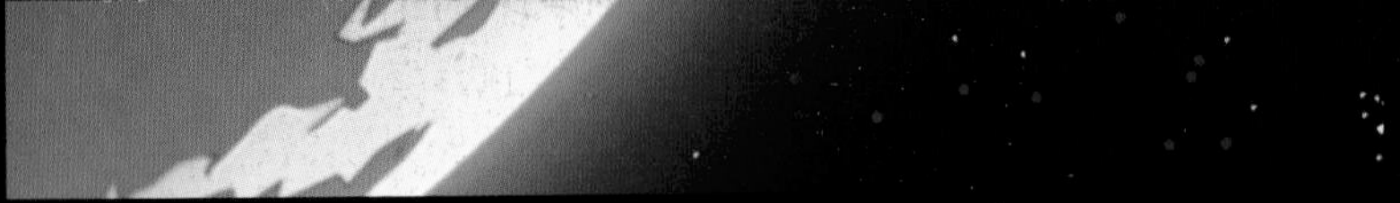

TABLE OF CONTENTS

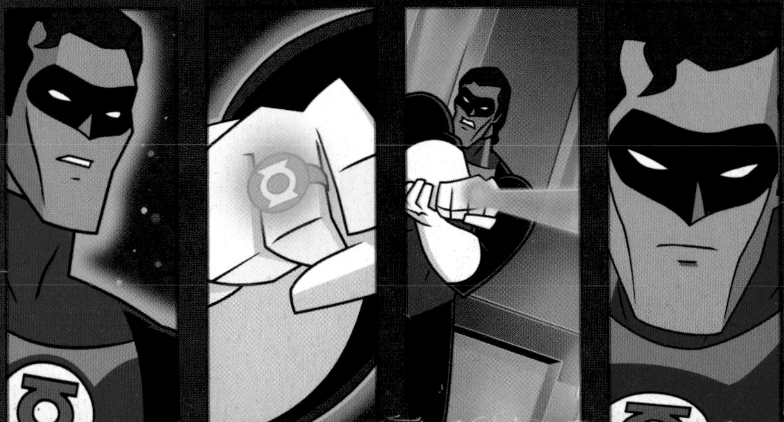

CHAPTER 1

SHARK ATTACK!

When he heard about trouble in his hometown of Coast City, Green Lantern Hal Jordan left the planet Oa as fast as possible. His adventures took him across the galaxy to planets covered in fiery volcanoes, icy forests, and even deserts. But there was no place that Hal cared about more than his home planet, Earth.

As he flew over the city, Hal saw people cheering him on. After all, Coast City was the "City Without Fear" — and Green Lantern was its protector.

"The source of the distress signal is at sea," said Hal's power ring.

"Offshore, huh?" asked Hal. "I didn't bring my bathing suit!"

Just then, Green Lantern spotted a pillar of smoke rising from the ocean. As he approached, Hal realized that a ship must have been wrecked there. Two people were in the water. They were splashing around and yelling for help.

Hal created a green life preserver with his ring and threw it toward the couple.

"Grab on!" Green Lantern shouted.

The man and woman each put an arm around the life preserver. Hal pulled them to safety.

"What was that thing that attacked our boat?!" cried the woman.

"I'm not sure," answered her friend. "But it looked like some kind of shark!"

A shark? thought Hal. *There's no way that a normal fish could have caused all this damage. It must be my enemy, the Shark!*

Hal looked carefully for any signs of the monstrous Shark, but he couldn't see him under the water's murky surface.

Suddenly, the Shark jumped out of the water and landed with a **THUD!** on the deck of a passing boat. He was a huge, muscular half-man, half-shark that could stand on two legs. He picked up the boat's captain and tossed him into the water as if he were as light as a skipping stone.

"Go fish!" growled the Shark, showing Hal his razor-sharp grin.

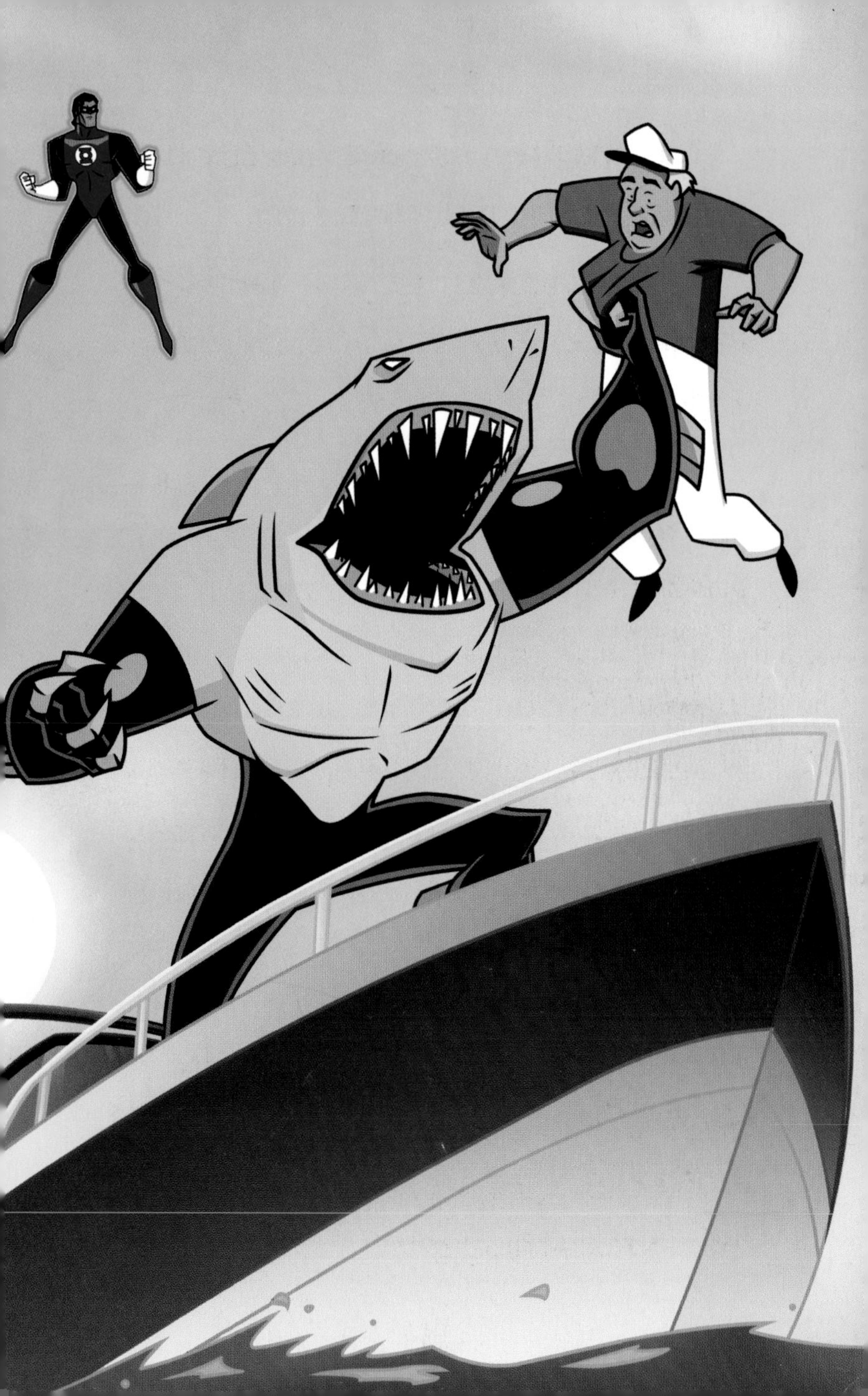

Green Lantern quickly constructed an emerald fishing rod with his ring. He flung it toward the boat captain. The captain grabbed onto the hook at the end of the construct and held on tight. Hal reeled the captain back to safety.

"Thanks!" said the captain. "Coast City can always count on Green Lantern!"

WHAM! WHAM! The Shark jumped up and down on the boat, smashing it to pieces. Then, he dived back into the water.

Hal knew he needed to stop the Shark before the villain caused any more trouble on the coast. He created a green fishing net with his ring and dropped it into the water at the very spot where the Shark had disappeared. After a few seconds, he felt a strong tug on the net, and pulled it from the water.

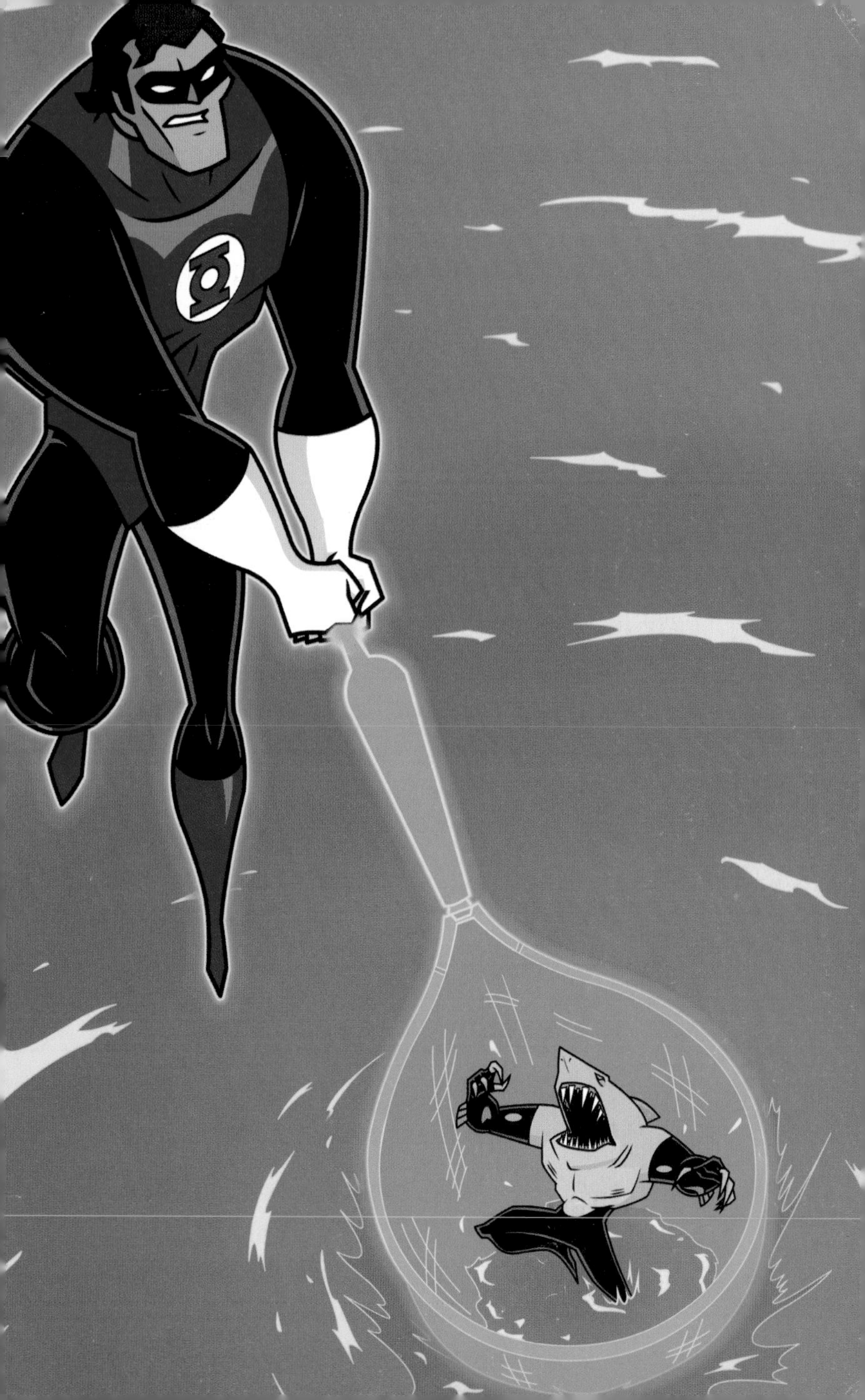

The Shark was trapped inside the net. The beast kicked and thrashed, but he was no match for the strength of Hal's will.

"So, what's it like to be the catch of the day?" Hal asked with a grin.

The Shark howled in frustration.

"Power levels at 10%," said Hal's ring.

"That should be more than enough to get this crook to jail . . . or at least to an empty tank at the aquarium," joked Hal.

*   *   *

A few hours later, Hal had just finished locking up the Shark in a special prison for super-villains. He was busy recharging his ring using his power battery when his ring alerted him.

"Incoming transmission," it said.

"Go ahead," said Hal.

A small image of the Green Lantern known as Fendor appeared from Hal's ring and began to speak. "Hal Jordan, my friend Sen-Tag and I are currently on your planet's moon," said the hologram. "We wish to inform you of a urgent mission and request your immediate help."

With the Shark locked up and Coast City safe, Hal had nothing else planned.

"You got it," the hero said. "I'll be right there."

CHAPTER 2

MEN ON THE MOON

Green Lantern was used to traveling through all sorts of dangerous places in outer space. A journey from Earth to the Moon would be easy.

"Ring, I'm going to take a quick nap. Wake me up when we're there," Hal said.

"Confirmed," replied the ring.

"Oh, and can you put my shields up, just in case?" asked Hal with a yawn.

"Alert: incoming asteroid!" cried Hal's ring. "Collision will occur in 1.2 seconds!"

"So much for that idea," said the Green Lantern, groggily.

A giant asteroid smashed into Hal's shields and shattered into a million tiny pieces. Green Lantern no longer felt sleepy.

"Caution! Shields damaged," Hal's ring informed him.

The hero puzzled over what to do. *I just need a way to destroy these rocks,* he thought. *What's the best way to go about clearing an asteroid field?*

Hal tried to think of how he would break down rocks if he were back on Earth. After a moment, he knew exactly what he needed — a jackhammer! He created a huge green jackhammer and started pounding away at the asteroids.

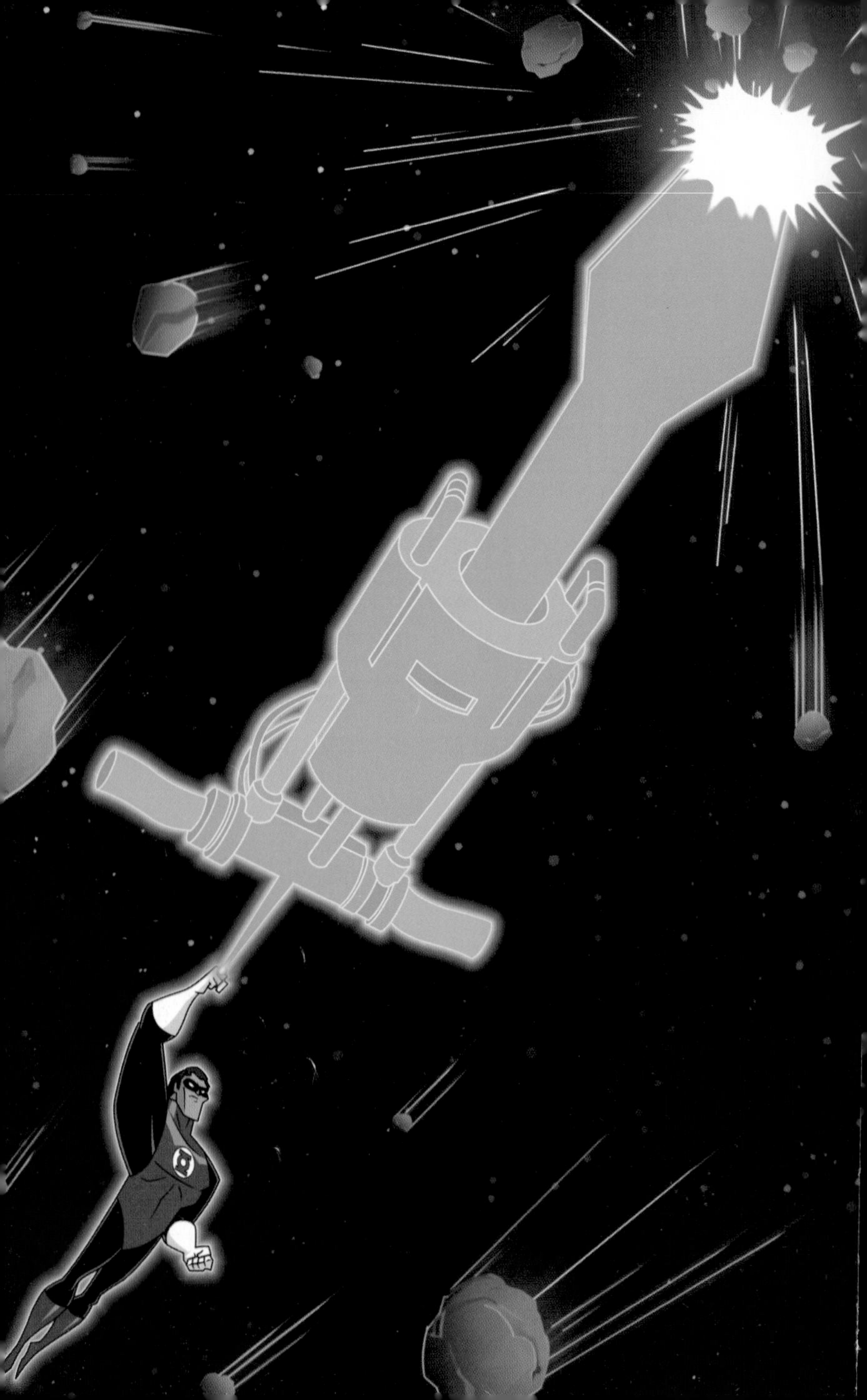

SMASH! SMASH! SMASH!

Hal swung the jackhammer at each asteroid. They were effortlessly demolished. One by one, the boulders broke into tiny stones that slowly drifted off into space. Hal had worked up a sweat, but he had managed to destroy every asteroid in sight.

"Well, if this whole 'Green Lantern' thing doesn't work out, I've got a bright future as a construction worker!" Hal said with a laugh.

"No additional asteroids within range," said Green Lantern's ring. "The space between your present location and the Moon is now clear."

"Thanks, ring," Hal said. "I suppose I should have checked for danger before I almost took a nap!"

Moments later, Hal flew over the dry, barren surface of the Moon. The Green Lantern spotted his fellow Corps members standing on the side of a large, sloping hill.

"Sorry for the delay. I had a little shark trouble," said Hal, landing next to Fendor and Sen-Tag. He shook their furry hands. "Welcome to the Moon, boys!"

Fendor looked confused. "Your planet's moon is not named?" he asked.

"Nope," answered Hal. "We just call it 'the Moon'."

"How very strange," said Sen-Tag. "Each one of our planet's fourteen moons has its own unique name."

"I would love to keep chatting, fellas," interrupted Hal, "but you made this mission sound pretty urgent."

"Ah, yes!" Fendor said. "Sorry for the delay, Hal Jordan."

"Recently, our rings received several distress calls from a nearby planet. Among them were reports of a massive explosion," explained Sen-Tag. He raised his ring and created a hologram of the troubled orb. "The disturbance came from this planet — the fourth one from your sun."

"You mean the Red Planet?" said Hal.

"This world is called the 'Red Planet'?" Fendor asked.

"Not exactly," replied Hal. "It's called Mars. It's nicknamed the Red Planet for its distinct color. What's happening there?"

"We are unsure," said Fendor. "After all, you are the Green Lantern most familiar with this Sector."

"You're right," said Hal. "And I'm happy to help. Are you guys ready to see some more of Sector 2814?"

"Yes, Hal Jordan!" the Green Lanterns shouted together.

ZWWWwOOOOMMMM!

Hal blasted off from the Moon. Fendor and Sen-Tag followed behind him.

"Red Planet, here we come!" shouted Hal, speeding toward Mars.

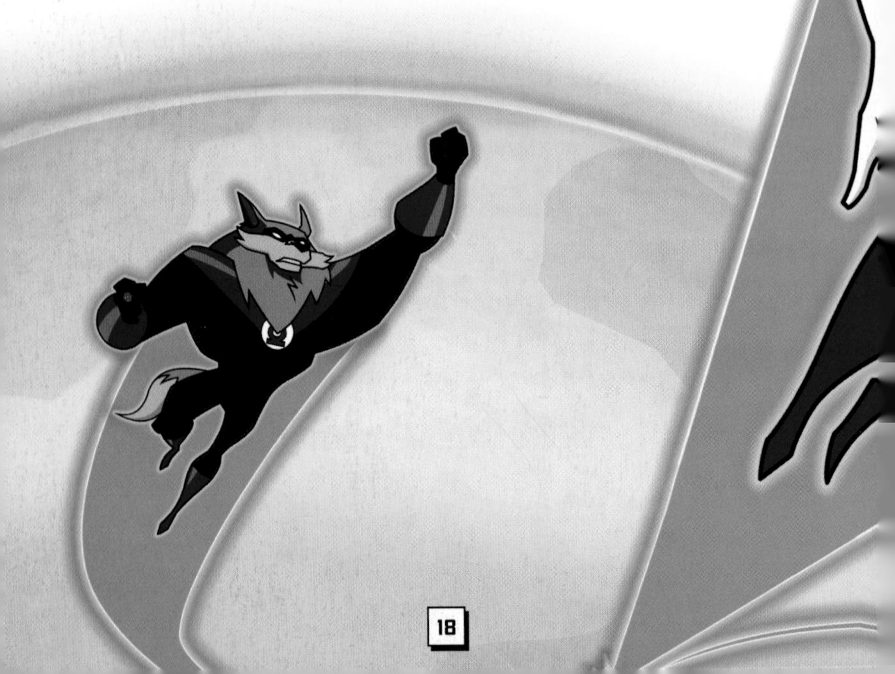

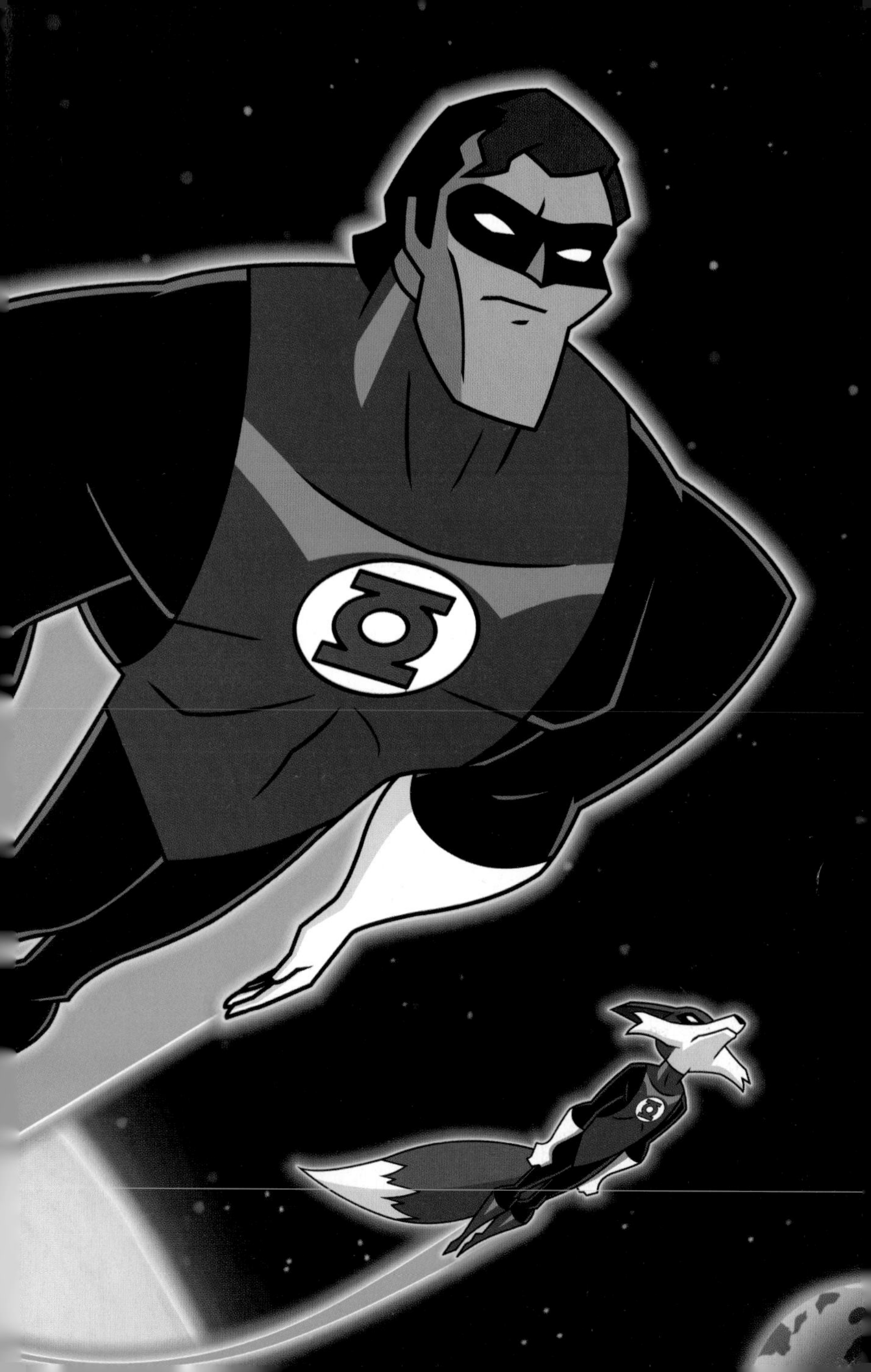

CHAPTER 3

MISSION TO MARS

As the Green Lanterns flew through the atmosphere of Mars, Fendor received another distress signal. **BEEP! BEEP!**

"Source of alarm located at the Mount Terra Mining Facility," explained his ring.

"A mining facility?" Fendor wondered. "That must be where the explosion took place. Something must have gone wrong."

"Or, they were attacked," added Sen-Tag.

"Either way, we have to make sure those miners are okay," said Hal.

When the Green Lanterns reached Mount Terra, they could immediately tell that something had indeed gone very wrong. Several mining trucks had been flipped upside down. The facility's radio tower had collapsed, and there was not a single miner in sight.

"This sure doesn't look like a simple accident!" Hal exclaimed.

Fendor pointed toward a cave in the side of a nearby mountain. "That must be the entrance to the facility," he said.

Hal nodded. "If they were attacked, the miners probably hid in there for safety," he said. "Let's go see if we can find them."

The Green Lanterns landed next to the entrance of the mining facility. The door was in place and seemed to be undamaged.

POW! POW! The Green Lanterns knocked loudly, but nobody answered.

"Ring, scan this area for additional life forms," said Fendor.

"Affirmative," said the ring. "Sixteen life forms are located inside the structure."

Hal knocked again. "Hello? Is anybody in there?" he repeated. "We're Green Lanterns responding to the distress signals."

Nothing but silence.

Sen-Tag's eyes went wide. "They could be trapped inside!" he cried.

"You're right!" said Hal. "We have to make sure they're okay. Stand back."

Hal constructed a chain saw with his ring. It quickly tore the door off of its hinges. **BZZZT!**

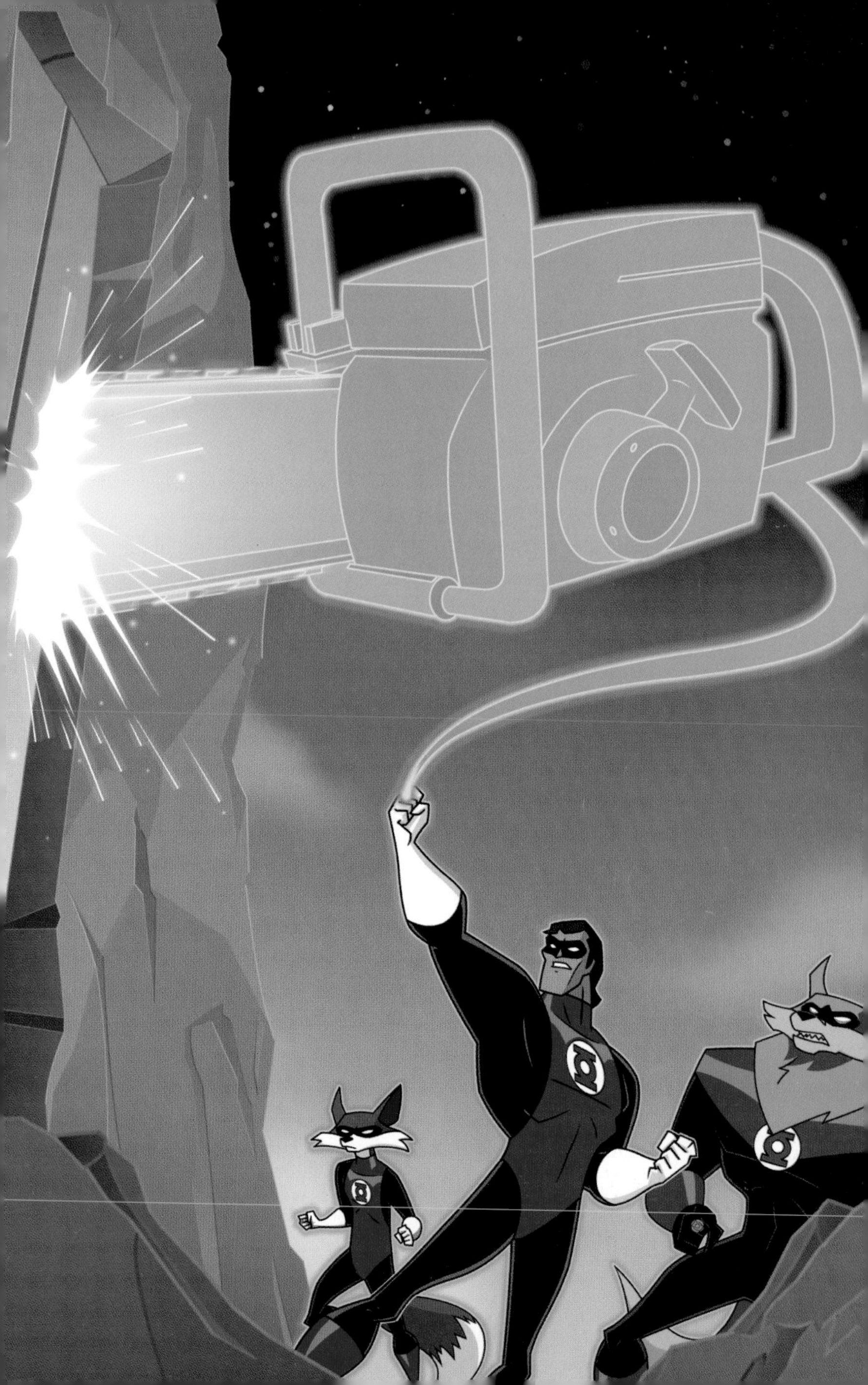

As the dust settled, Hal and the other Green Lanterns spotted several miners huddled together at the back of the facility. Emergency breathing devices had kept them all alive, but the men were shaking with fright.

"What happened here?" asked Hal.

"M-monsters!" stammered one of the men. "R-red m-monsters!"

Fendor spun around, searching for any signs of the attackers. "Did you see where they went?" he asked.

"Over that ridge," replied one of the miners. He pointed outside of the entrance toward a rocky hill on the horizon.

"Don't worry," said Hal. "We'll find out who is responsible for this!"

The Green Lanterns took off. As they flew over the ridge, the trio quickly spotted a series of massive canals dug into the planet's surface. The sand surrounding the ditches had been scorched by flames.

"Who could have done this?" Fendor asked Hal.

Hal hovered above the surface, studying the pattern and placement of the canals. The outer ditches formed a circle. Inside of this ring, Hal thought he recognized a familiar symbol.

Hal shot into the sky like a rocket.

"Where are you going?" asked Fendor. He and Sen-Tag followed closely behind.

"To answer your question," replied Hal.

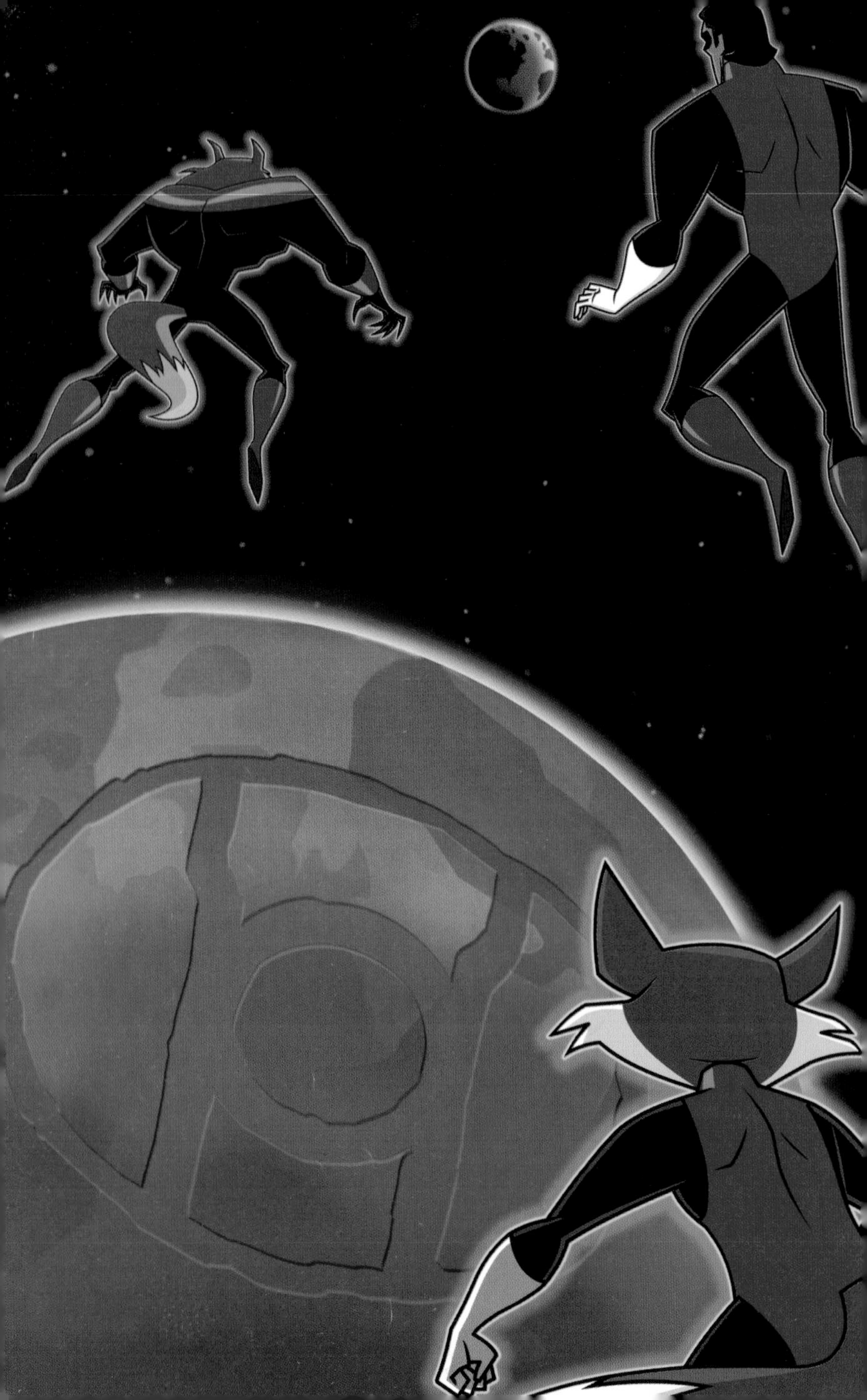

High in the air, Hal looked down at the planet once more. From up in the sky, Hal could see the pattern clearly.

"The symbol of the Red Lanterns!" said Hal. "They must have attacked the miners!"

"But why?" asked Fendor.

"I don't know. Nothing valuable has ever been found in these mines," replied the Green Lantern. "However, this mission was surely motivated by anger. It is the only emotion that fuels the Red Lanterns."

"Maybe it's best to avoid them," said Sen-Tag. "The attack seems to be over."

"Yes, for now," interrupted Hal. "But no doubt, their evil intentions run deep. We must go to the planet Ysmault, locate their leader, Atrocitus, and determine the root cause of this attack."

"Won't that be a dangerous mission?" asked Fendor.

"We're not going there for a fight," Hal assured his friends. "But we need to figure out why the Red Lanterns launched this attack on Mars."

"You are always so brave, Hal Jordan," said Sen-Tag. "We would be honored to accompany you to Ysmault."

Hal smiled. "I could definitely use the backup!" he admitted. "Now, let's go!"

CHAPTER 4

THE RED LANTERNS

Soon, the Green Lanterns were soaring above Ysmault. The planet was covered in erupting volcanoes and rivers and lakes of bubbling red liquid. The heroes flew over hundreds of ancient tree trunks, but none of the plants appeared to be alive.

"This way," said Hal. He flew ahead of the other Green Lanterns. "Their headquarters is straight ahead."

Fendor and Sen-Tag followed closely behind. Finally, Hal stopped in midair and pointed to the ground below.

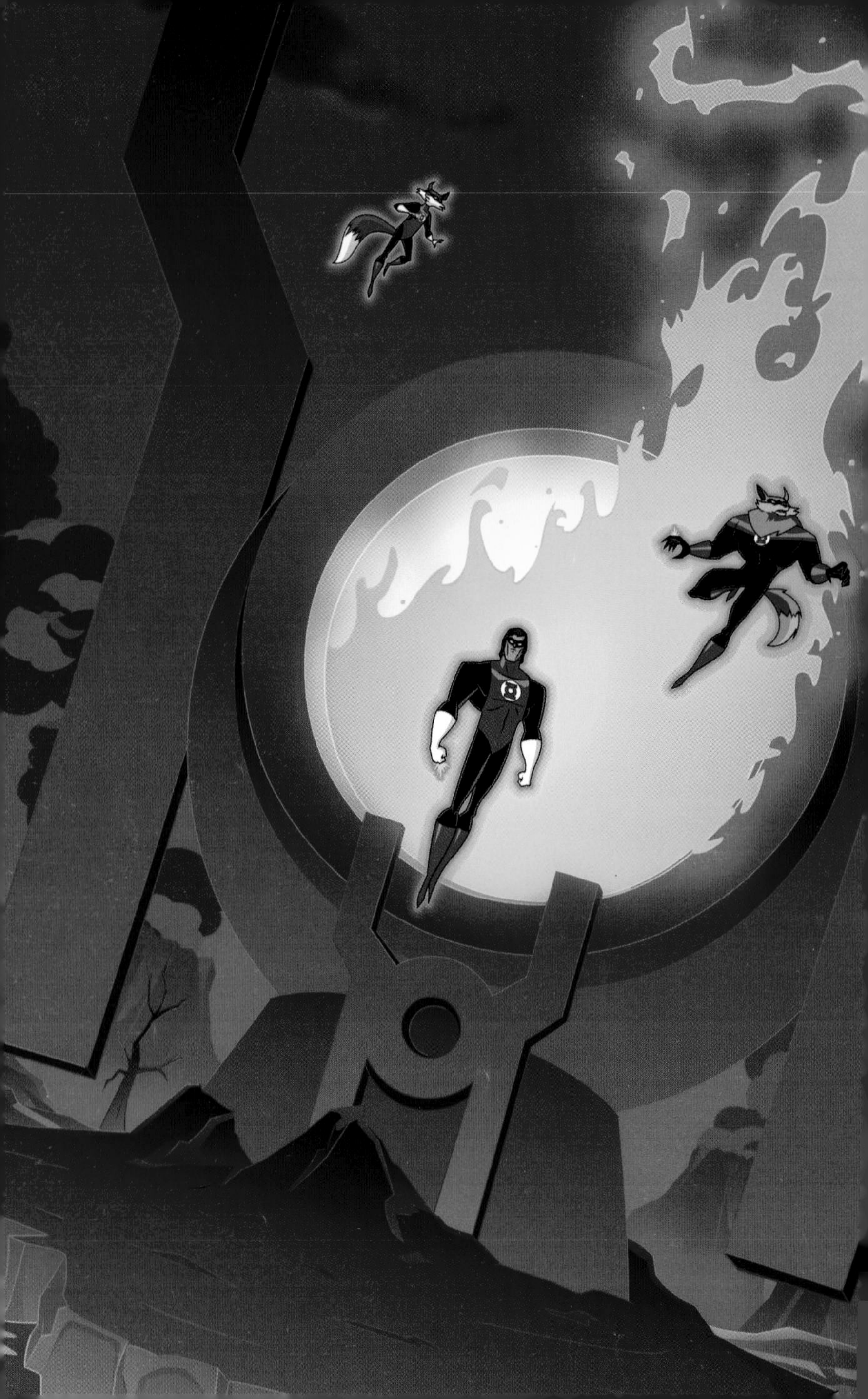

A gigantic building sat in a pool of the bubbling red liquid. It was surrounded by several smaller structures, all shaped like the symbol of the Red Lantern.

"This is it," said Hal. He landed on the ground beside the red pool. "Atrocitus and his Red Lanterns should be nearby. Let's split up and search the planet."

"Good idea," said Fendor.

"You two stick together and head north," added Hal. "I'll scope out this area for signs of danger. Stay in touch, and be safe!"

As Fendor and Sen-Tag flew off, Hal zeroed in on the Red Lantern headquarters. As he neared the giant red building, Hal expected to be attacked by its guards. Instead, the surrounding area was eerily quiet.

That's odd, thought Hal. Although the strange silence concerned him, the hero wasn't deterred. He needed to find out what the Red Lanterns were planning — even if that meant putting his life in danger.

Peeking inside the facility, Hal knew he had made the right decision. Several Red Lanterns sat at a briefing table. They studied images of Mars on a giant projection screen. The evil aliens seemed to be debating something of great importance.

Trying to hear their arguments, Hal poked his head into the room.

BEEP! BEEP! BEEP!

Suddenly, an alarm sounded from Hal's ring. "Green Lanterns Fendor and Sen-Tag have activated their distress beacons," announced the device.

Hal looked up from his ring. "Uh-oh," he exclaimed.

Every Red Lantern in the conference room had also been alerted by the alarm. The aliens rose from their chairs. Some growled with anger as they made their way toward the Green Lantern.

"Excuse me, fellas. I didn't mean to interrupt," said Hal. "Carry on."

Hal spun around and prepared to escape into the sky. WHAM! Instead, the fist of an angry beast slammed into Hal's chest.

Hal stumbled backward. He fell to the ground, dazed by the unexpected blow.

When he looked up, Hal saw the leader of the Red Lanterns standing over him.

"Atrocitus!" shouted the hero.

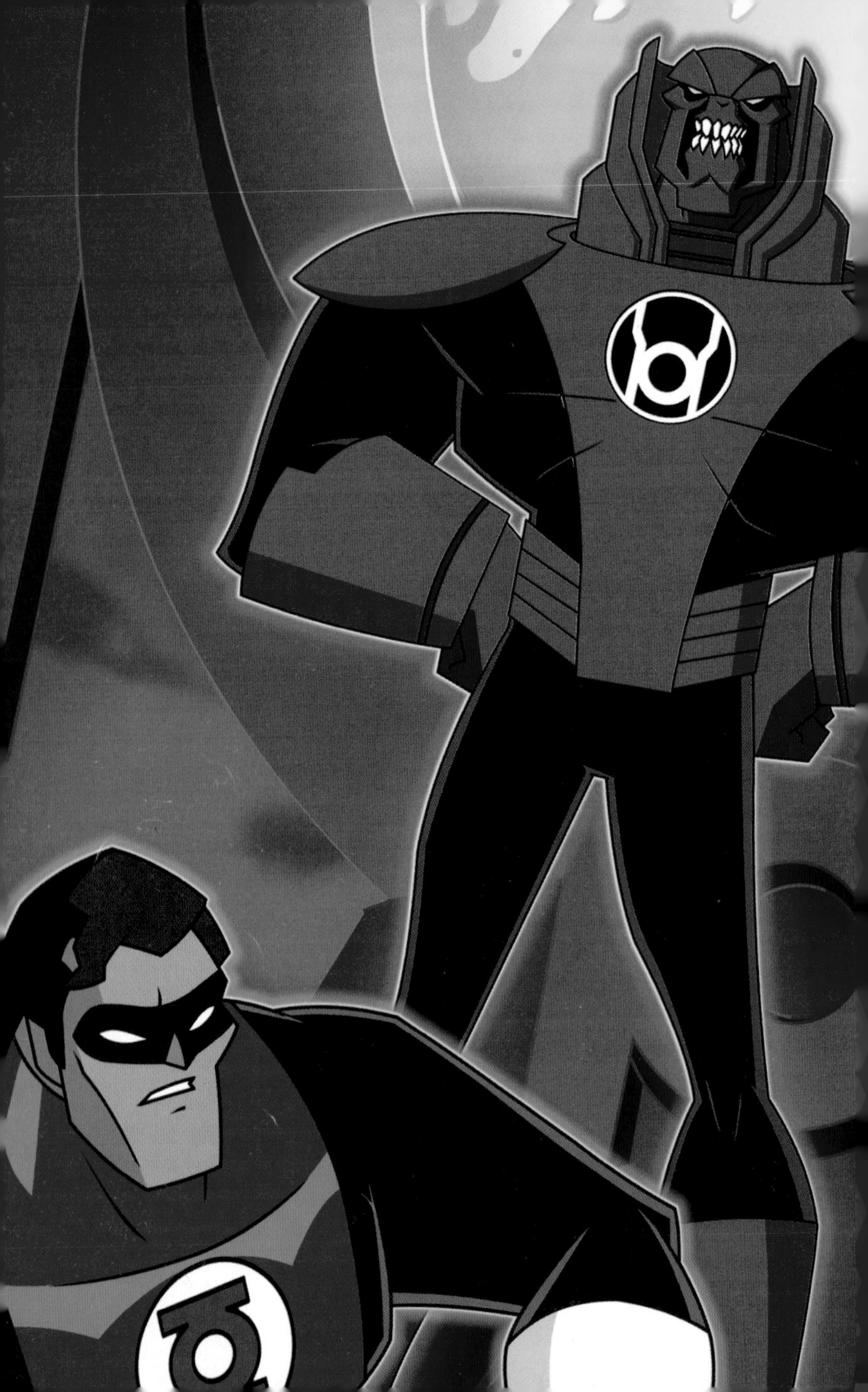

"You're not leaving us, are you?" asked the skull-faced beast. "We can't start our meeting without the guest of honor."

Atrocitus looked up. Then he stared back down at Hal and smiled. "Or should I say *guests*?" said the evil leader with a laugh.

Two more Red Lanterns floated down from the sky. Fendor and Sen-Tag were dragged behind them in a glowing red cage. The Red Lanterns had created this prison with their powerful rings.

"Take them inside!" Atrocitus told his underlings. "We have matters to discuss."

The guards placed Hal inside the cage with Fendor and Sen-Tag. Then, they dragged the cell into their headquarters. Inside, angry aliens stood around a table, snarling at the arrival of their enemies.

"What are they doing here?!" shouted a Red Lantern named Bleez. "These intruders must be destroyed!"

"Patience!" said Atrocitus. "Remember, all *bad* things come to those who wait."

The room let out a knowing laugh. Then the guards placed the cage with its prisoners near the head of the briefing table. All the Red Lanterns took their seats, and their attention turned toward the front of the room. The hateful leader stood at a podium, prepared to speak.

"Welcome," Atrocitus began. "As you all know, the power of the Red Lanterns grows throughout the universe. But as we expand, so must our empire. For years, we have searched for new planets, new worlds to stake our claim. And today, we have found something horrendously wonderful!"

Atrocitus turned and pointed to the screen behind him. On it, an image of Mars appeared, scarred with the Red Lantern symbol. The room erupted in applause.

"Never!" Hal cried out. "You won't find a home in my solar system!"

"Ha!" laughed Atrocitus. "Yes, on the surface, your Red Planet looks like a habitable place for my kind. But I'm not interested in what's on the surface. My interests are much deeper than that."

A new image appeared on the screen. It showed a cross-section of Mars. Far below the surface were several frozen reservoirs.

"Water?" Hal wondered aloud. "You couldn't possibly have a need for that resource."

"We don't," said Atrocitus, "but *you* do."

The image on the screen changed again. It now showed a picture of Earth. The planet's vast oceans sparkled with sunlight.

"Since we last fought, I've learned a few things," continued the Red Lantern leader. "First, there is no planet you care about more than Earth. Second, your planet is dying. Within a generation, your kind will have polluted the one resource you can't live without — water. And when it is gone, you will search for other nearby sources. Unfortunately, I have already found them."

"But why?" questioned Hal. "Why cripple one measly planet, when there's trillions more to be conquered?"

"Simple," replied Atrocitus. "To watch you suffer. You see, the other thing I learned is that anger is a treat, but nothing's sweeter than lasting REVENGE!"

CHAPTER 5

ANGER MANAGEMENT

"We'll see about that!" said Hal. He created a crowbar and pried open the bars on the red cage. He and the other Green Lanterns escaped. "You're not going to hurt us or anyone else in this galaxy!"

"It has already begun," yelled Atrocitus. "My Red Lantern Corps will return to Mars and drain its precious resource. Your planet's last hope will be drained as well!"

Atrocitus' eyes glowed red with anger. The evil alien opened his mouth, and flaming red liquid shot out.

Hal rolled out of the way, and the liquid hit a nearby chair.

WHOOOOSH! It burst into flames.

"You forgot to tell us that they could breathe fire!" Sen-Tag said to Hal.

Hal spun toward his friends. "Sorry about that!" replied the hero, ducking behind the briefing table. "The Red Lanterns can shoot a powerful red plasma. It's hotter than fire, so watch out!"

Fendor smiled weakly. "It's a little late for that," he said.

"Quiet, cowards!" boomed Atrocitus. "Dex-Starr, silence them!"

A small cat with long fangs and a Red Lantern uniform crawled out from behind Sen-Tag.

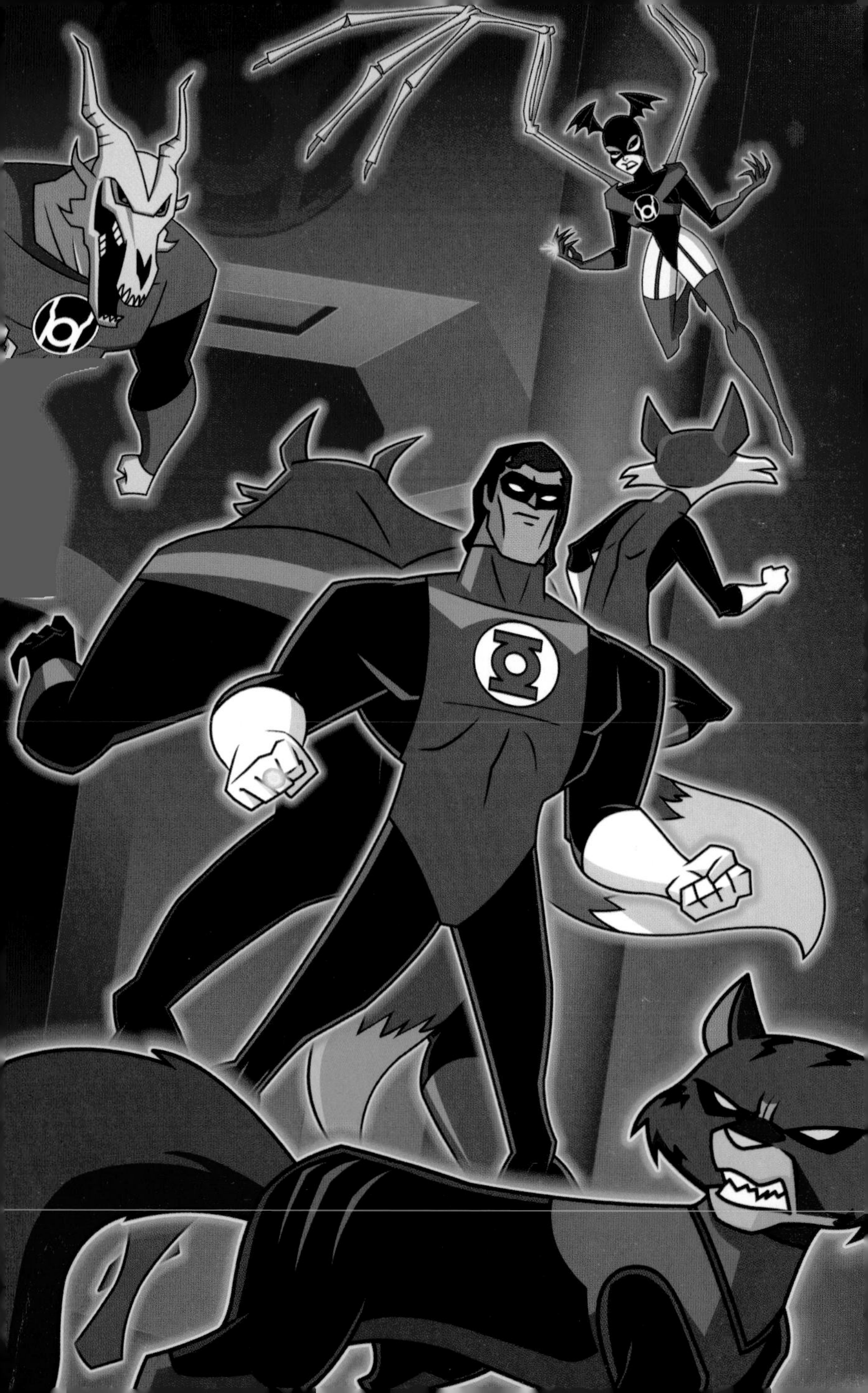

The evil cat spewed red plasma toward Fendor and Sen-Tag.

Hal quickly created a lasso with his ring. He spun it in the air, and tossed it at Dex-Starr. The cat tried to run, but the lasso landed right around its neck.

"You should really keep this kitty on a leash," Hal joked.

Hal tied the other end of the lasso to the table. "Stay!" he commanded the cat.

With the leash on, Dex-Starr could no longer reach Sen-Tag or Fendor. They were safe — for now.

When Atrocitus saw what Hal had done, he ordered the other Red Lanterns to attack. Several of the angry beasts raced toward Hal and his friends.

Each one spat fiery red liquid from its mouth.

WHOOOOSH!

Hal quickly made a shield with his ring. He protected himself from the lava-like liquid. With his other hand, Hal created a laser blaster. He fired off a few shots at each of the Red Lanterns.

ZZAPPPPPP!

The evil beasts dodged the hero's blasts.

"What do we do, brave hero?" Sen-Tag asked Hal from across the room. "You instructed us not to fight them."

"Change of plans!" shouted Hal.

Just then, Skallox, a Red Lantern with the face of a dragon and the body of a man, crashed into Fendor.

The Lanterns tumbled to the ground.

The monster screamed.

Fendor threw the creature off of him. He created a giant green sword with his power ring and slashed at the dragon with all his might. Skallox blasted the sword with plasma, eroding it before Fendor could strike. The beast would not be slayed.

Meanwhile, a female Red Lantern with skeleton wings swooped down from the sky. She grabbed Hal with her razor-sharp claws. Another Red Lantern that looked like a giant jellyfish wrapped Sen-Tag in its tentacles. He tried to escape using his ring.

"Our constructs are not working!" Sen-Tag exclaimed. "They are burning right through them!"

Hal wrestled his way out of his attacker's claws. The hero climbed onto her back and grabbed hold of her skeletal wings. He sent the beast flying into the evil jellyfish.

The Red Lanterns fell to the ground, allowing Hal and Sen-Tag to escape.

Hal thought back to his battle against the Shark in Coast City. "Fendor! Sen-Tag!" he shouted. "We need a net!"

"A what?!" questioned Fendor. Sen-Tag looked puzzled as well.

"Our individual constructs aren't enough to defeat these beasts," explained Hal. "But together, we can create a barrier strong enough to contain them."

"We're behind you, Hal Jordan," shouted Fendor. "Lead the way!"

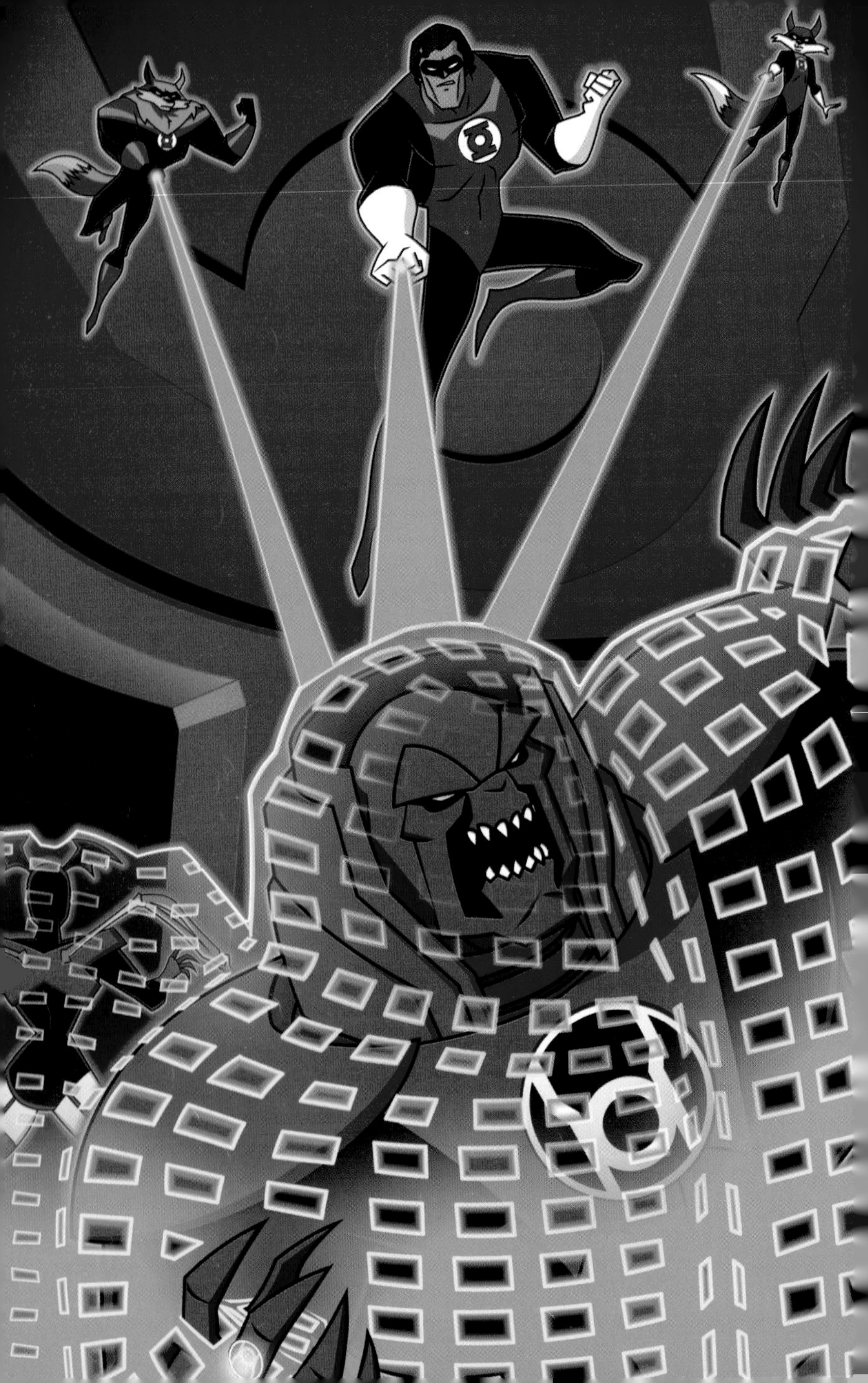

The Green Lanterns soared around and around the Red Lanterns as quickly as they could.

ZWWWOOOOMMMMM!

Each one wrapped their enemies in green netting. Then the heroes came together. They combined their restraints into one gigantic net. All the Red Lanterns were trapped inside.

"It won't hold for long," said Fendor.

"Then we must hurry!" Hal replied.

Using every ounce of willpower, the Green Lanterns lifted the enormous net. They carried it out of the Red Lantern headquarters, over the blood-red moats, and toward a cavern in one of the planet's many volcanoes. The Green Lanterns heaved the net inside the deep pit.

"They'll stay on Ysmault!" Hal said to his fellow Green Lanterns. "If I see any Red Lanterns in my sector, I'll lock them up in the Sciencell prisons."

"AAAAARG!" Atrocitus growled.

Remembering how he had destroyed the asteroids earlier, Hal created another giant jackhammer. This time he motioned for his super hero friends to follow. Together, they blasted at the rocks outside the cavern. Soon, the entrance was completely covered with a hundred tons of boulders.

"Since you like mining so much," Hal shouted through the rock barrier, "let's see you dig your way out of this!"

The cave would hold them long enough for Hal to establish security on Mars. He would protect the Red Planet at any cost.

With their enemies contained, Hal and the other Green Lanterns left Ysmault. They began the long flight back to Mars.

"Do you believe what Atrocitus said, Hal?" asked Fendor as the group soared toward the Milky Way Galaxy. "Will humans destroy all water on Earth?"

"I'm not sure," replied Hal. "But they will decide that fate, not some hot-headed madman. And until then, I plan on protecting and enjoying my planet's most precious resource."

"Even the shark infested parts?" joked Sen-Tag.

"Yes, my friend," answered Hal. "Every last drop."

ATROCITUS

REAL NAME: Atrocitus

OCCUPATION: Founder and leader of the Red Lanterns Corps

EYES: Yellow   **HAIR:** None

POWERS/ABILITIES: Superhuman strength and durability; razor-sharp claws and teeth; flight; power ring creates hard-light projections of anything imaginable.

BIOGRAPHY

Long ago, an interstellar police force known as the Manhunters ravaged Atrocitus' home planet, destroying everything in sight and leaving only five beings alive. Atrocitus and the other four survivors formed the Five Inversions. This group set out to eradicate the Guardians of the Universe, who they blamed for the creation of the Manhunters and the destruction of their planet. Their plans quickly failed, and the Green Lanterns imprisoned Atrocitus and the others in Ysmault. There, a violent rage grew inside Atrocitus. He destroyed the other survivors, created the Red Lantern Corps from the power of his victims, and vowed revenge against the Green Lanterns Corps.

2814

The Red Lantern Corps is based on Ysmault. This desolate red planet is located in Sector 2814, the area of space Hal Jordan protects.

After forming the Red Lantern Corps, Atrocitus sent power rings to other evil beings, including Abyssma, Antipathy, Bleez, Dex-Starr, Fury-6, Haggor, Ratchet, Skallox, and Zilius Zox.

After accepting the power rings, the hearts of the new Red Lantern Corps members filled with rage and became useless. An awful red plasma spilled from their mouths, burning everything it touched.

Each Lantern color is powered by an emotion: Green Lanterns are fueled by willpower; Blue Lanterns get their energy from hope; Orange Lanterns thrive on greed; and Red Lanterns feed off of anger.

BIOGRAPHIES

Michael Acampora was born in the Bronx, New York. He has edited various books and magazines for DC Comics and is currently pursuing degrees in Literary Arts and Political Science at Brown University. He splits his time living with his family in Somers, New York, and friends in Providence, Rhode Island.

Dan Schoening was born in Victoria, B.C., Canada. From an early age, Dan has had a passion for animation and comic books. Currently, Dan does freelance work in the animation and game industry and spends a lot of time with his lovely little daughter, Paige.

GLOSSARY

affirmative (uh-FUR-muh-tiv)—giving the answer "yes," or stating something is true

asteroid (ASS-tuh-roid)—small chunks of rock that travel through space. Asteroids are most common between Earth and Jupiter.

atmosphere (AT-muhss-fihr)—the mixture of gases that surrounds a planet

beacon (BEE-kuhn)—a light used as a signal or warning

deterred (di-TURD)—discouraged or prevented something

galaxy (GAL-uhk-see)—a very large group of stars and planets

hologram (HOL-uh-gram)—an image made by laser beams that looks three-dimensional

intentions (in-TEN-shuhnz)—things that a person means to do

willpower (WIL-pou-ur)—the ability to choose and control what you will and will not do

DISCUSSION QUESTIONS

1. Sen-Tag and Fendor helped Hal take down the Red Lantern Corps. Do you think Hal could have defeated them alone? Why or why not?

2. Hal's ring is fueled by willpower. If you had a power ring, what emotion or feeling would you want to fuel your powers? Discuss your answers.

3. Do you think the Red Lanterns will attack Mars again? Explain your answer.

WRITING PROMPTS

1. Write another chapter to this book. How will Green Lantern protect the water supply on Mars? How will he keep Earth safe from Red Lanterns in the future? You decide.

2. Create your own Lantern Corps. What color are their rings? What part of the universe do they come from? Are they heroes or villains?

3. If you had Hal's power ring, what would you do with it? Would you fight crime and protect the universe? What would you fight for? Write about your life as a super hero.

MORE NEW GREEN LANTERN ADVENTURES!

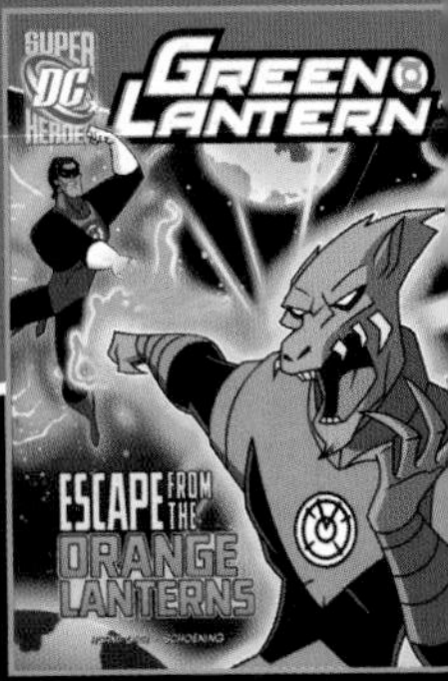
SUPER DC HEROES
GREEN LANTERN
ESCAPE FROM THE ORANGE LANTERNS

ESCAPE FROM THE ORANGE LANTERNS

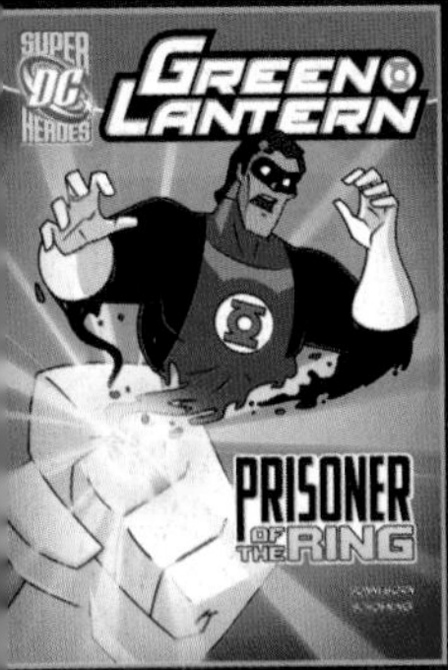
SUPER DC HEROES
GREEN LANTERN
PRISONER OF THE RING

PRISONER OF THE RING

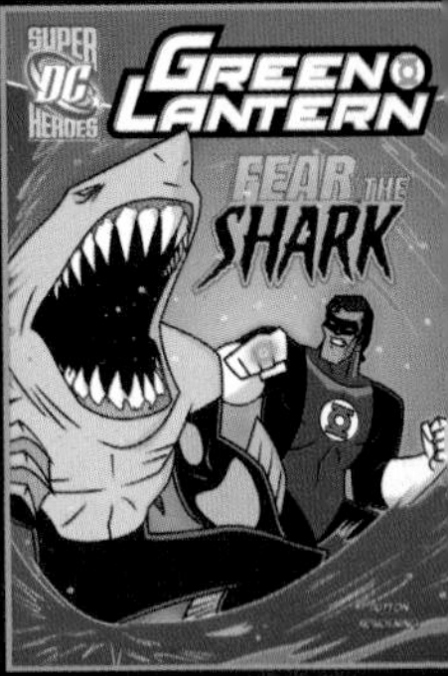
SUPER DC HEROES
GREEN LANTERN
FEAR THE SHARK

FEAR THE SHARK

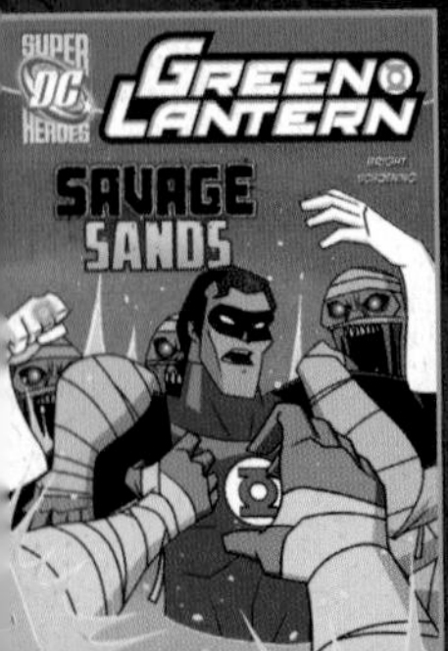
SUPER DC HEROES
GREEN LANTERN
SAVAGE SANDS

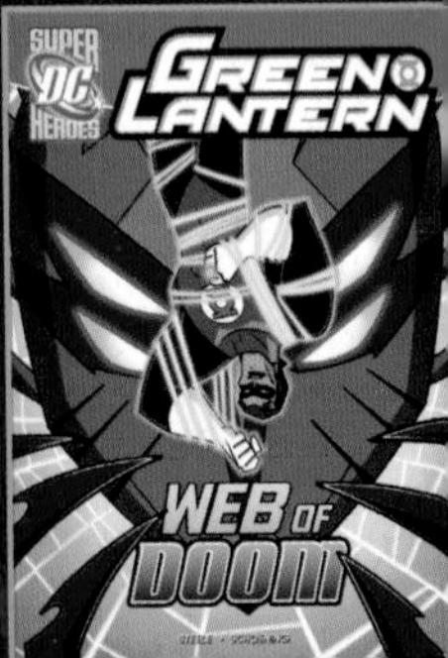
SUPER DC HEROES
GREEN LANTERN
WEB OF DOOM

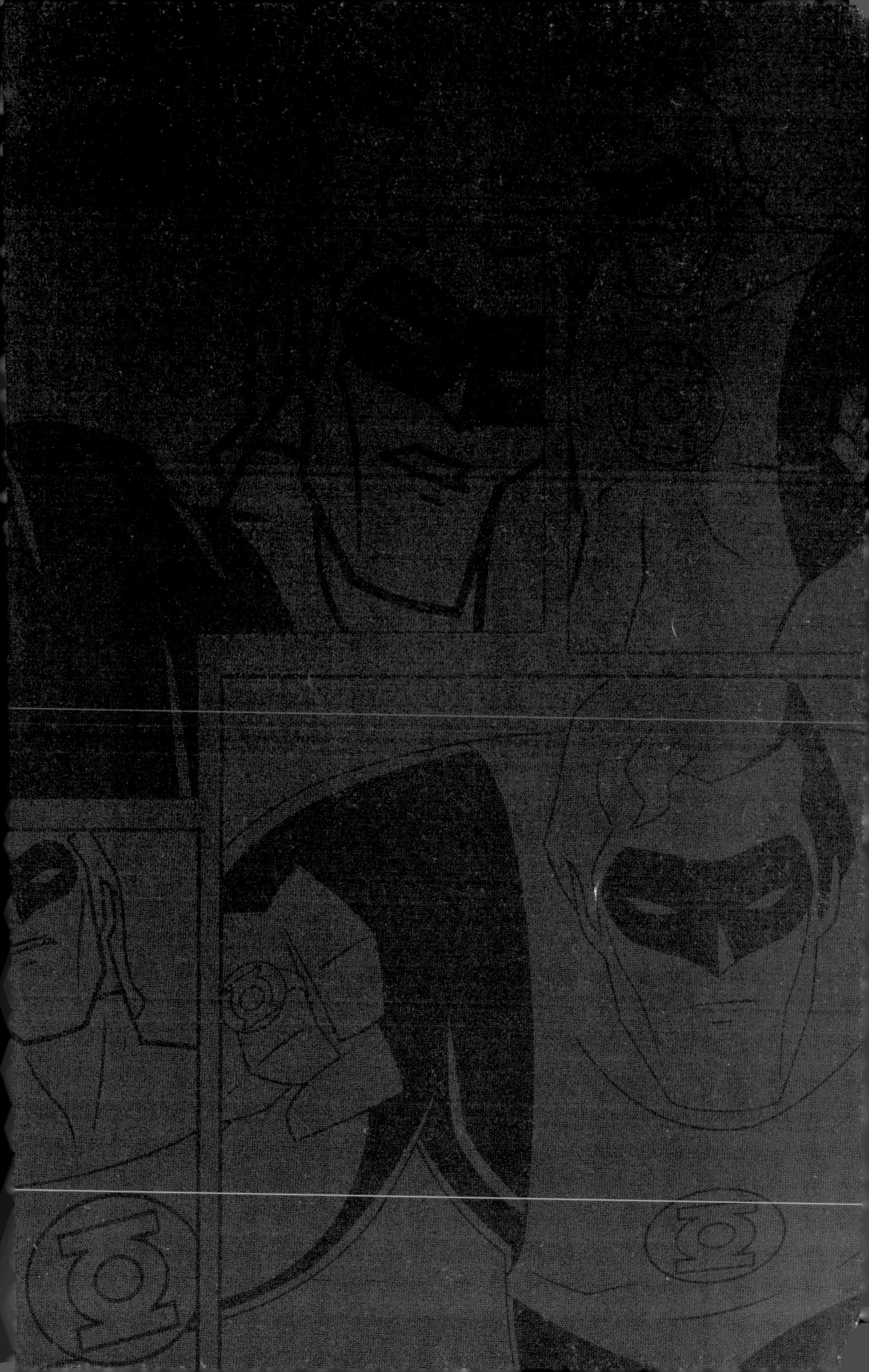

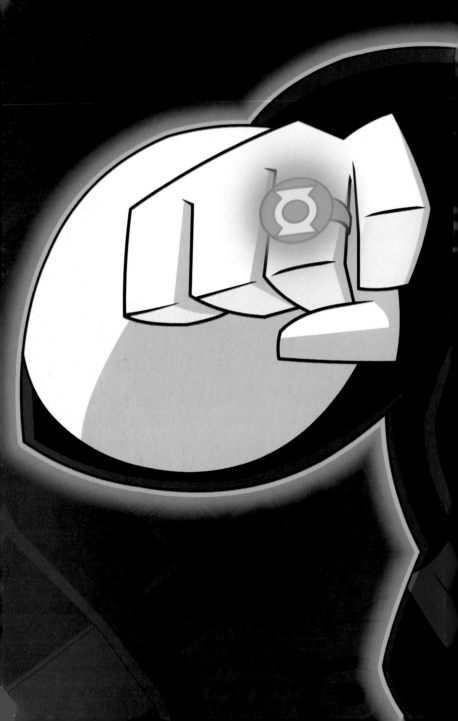

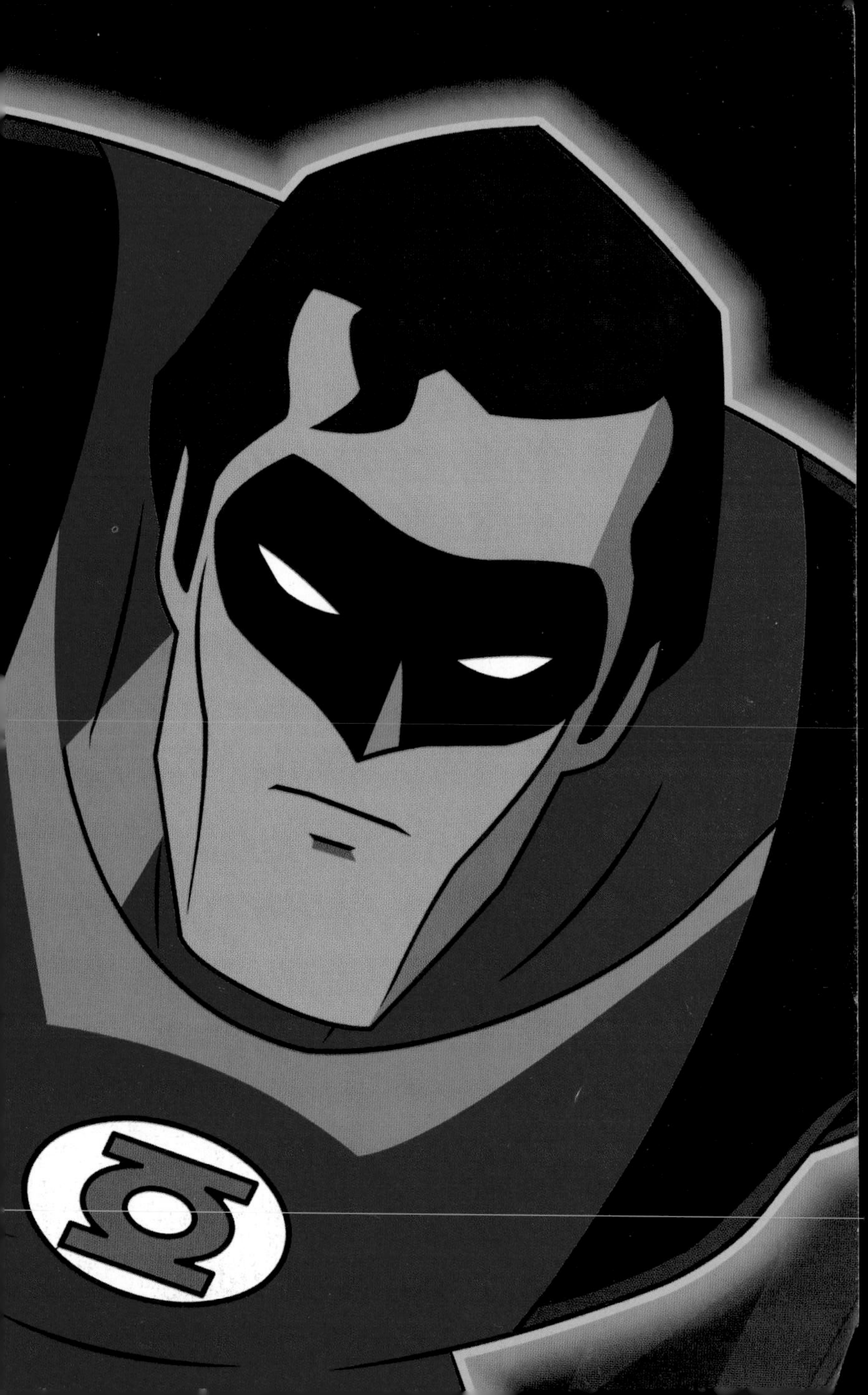